To Nan, the master snacker
— E.L.

For Kate, Queen of Snacks
— D.B.

Text copyright © 1995 by Elizabeth Levy.
Illustrations copyright © 1995 by Denise Brunkus.
All rights reserved. Published by Scholastic Inc.
Printed in the U.S.A.
ISBN 0-590-06681-1
HELLO READER!, CARTWHEEL BOOKS, and the CARTWHEEL BOOKS logo are registered trademarks of Scholastic Inc.

9 10   23   03 02 01 00

INVISIBLE INC. #3

The Snack Attack Mystery

by Elizabeth Levy

Illustrated by Denise Brunkus

Hello Reader! Lincoln School Library

SCHOLASTIC INC.

New York Toronto London Auckland Sydney

Chip fell into a strange pool of water. Now Chip is invisible! Justin knows how to read lips because of his hearing loss. Charlene is sometimes bossy, but always brave. Together they are Invisible Inc.— and they solve mysteries!

CHAPTER 1
A Very, Very Weird Class

Chip stood very still. He tried to be quiet. But his stomach growled. He hoped nobody could hear it. He didn't want anyone to find him.

Chip and his friends were playing hide-and-seek. They had to make new rules because he was invisible: (1) Chip couldn't hide behind trees. (2) Chip couldn't hold his breath. (3) Chip couldn't leave the playground.

Chip's stomach growled again.

"I think I heard something," said Charlene. She waved her hands in the air. She hoped to find Chip first.

Chip tried to make his stomach quiet. But he was really hungry.

"I hear him!" Charlene shouted. Charlene lunged. She came up with nothing but air.

Her little brother, Stanley, laughed. "You couldn't even catch *me*. And *I'm* not even invisible."

Stanley twirled by. He almost twirled right into Chip.

"This isn't a game for kindergartners," Charlene said to her brother.

"You don't have to be mean to him," said Justin.

Charlene rolled her eyes. "You don't know him. Now, I've forgotten where I heard Chip's stomach."

Just then, their teacher, Mr. Gonshak, came outside with a new girl.

"Boys and girls, gather around," said Mr. Gonshak. "This is Dawn Park. She is new to our class. Charlene, why don't you let Dawn play in your game?"

Mr. Gonshak went to talk to the other teachers.

"Hi, Dawn," said Charlene. "We're playing hide-and-seek. You can help Sandy and Justin and me catch Chip. I know he's close. His noisy stomach is going to give him away."

Charlene waved her arms in the air. Justin and Sandy waved, too.

"What are you doing?" Dawn asked.

"We're looking for Chip," said Sandy. "He's around here somewhere."

Dawn turned around. "I don't see any hiding places," she said.

"Chip doesn't need a hiding place. He's invisible," explained Justin.

Dawn thought that the children were making fun of her. She hated going to a new school. She hated not having friends.

Just then Chip's stomach growled again. Charlene heard it. She grabbed the air and got Chip's arm.

"I got him!" she shouted.

"This is so embarrassing!" said Chip.

The air around his face got red.

"Over here, Dawn!" shouted Charlene. "We got him."

Dawn looked at Charlene. Charlene was talking to somebody who wasn't there.

"Isn't she a little old to have an imaginary friend?" Dawn asked Justin.

"What?" said Justin.

"Isn't she a little old to have an imaginary friend?" Dawn shouted.

"You have to face me. I can read lips," said Justin.

"Dawn, meet Chip," Charlene said.

She pointed to the air beside her.

Dawn started to cry. She thought that everyone was teasing her.

Just then Mr. Gonshak blew his whistle.

"It's time to come in," he said. "Chip, go change into your regular clothes."

"Good," said a voice next to Dawn. "It's snack time. I'm starving."

Dawn jumped. "Who said that?"

"Me! I'm Chip!" said Chip.

He reached out and shook Dawn's hand. She felt something—but she saw nothing. Dawn screamed.

"What's wrong?" shouted Mr. Gonshak.

"The new girl is afraid of Chip!" said Keith. He laughed.

"Dawn, we'll tell you about Chip during snack time," said Mr. Gonshak.

"Mr. Gonshak's hungry," said Justin. "He was just talking to the teachers about being on a diet."

"How do you know what he said all the way over there?" asked Dawn.

"I've got ways," said Justin proudly.

Justin's teacher spoke into a microphone. It made his teacher's voice sound louder just to Justin. Mr. Gonshak was always forgetting to turn it off.

Dawn blinked. Everyone was trying to confuse her.

The boys and girls walked into the classroom. They went to their cubbies to get their snacks. Except for Dawn.

"I didn't bring a snack," said Dawn. "No one told me to."

"You can have some of mine," said Sandy.

But Sandy couldn't find her snack. "Hey!" she shouted. "My snack is gone! I had a bag of nuts and raisins."

"Mine is gone, too!" said Charlene.

"So is mine!" said Justin.

His mom had packed his favorite — chocolate-covered nuts.

Just then Dawn screamed. She saw a shirt, pants, and shoes — but no head or hands. Chip had walked in the door.

Chip went to his cubby.

"My snack! Somebody took my snack!" he said.

"This is a case for Invisible Inc.," said Justin loudly.

"What's Invisible Inc.?" asked Dawn. She was almost crying. It was her first day in a brand-new school, and nothing made sense at all.

Mr. Gonshak tried to explain. "One of the boys in this class is a little different. We have gotten used to Chip. But it can be a shock when you first meet him. Chip, please tell Dawn what happened to you."

Chip walked to the front of the class, brushing against Dawn. Dawn shivered as if he were a ghost. Chip told her what had happened to him.

Charlene waved her arm in the air. "Mr. Gonshak! Mr. Gonshak! Let me tell Dawn about Invisible Inc."

"It's a club with a boy you can't see, a boy who can't hear, and a girl who bosses everybody around!" Keith shouted out.

The class laughed.

Mr. Gonshak frowned at Keith. He pointed to the bulletin board.

CLASS RULES
1. No shouting out in class.
2. No calling each other names.

MOTTO

"Keith, remember our class rules. No shouting out in class. No calling each other names." Mr. Gonshak turned to the class. "What is our motto?"

"Respect for ourselves and each other!" said the class.

Dawn felt more confused than ever. And she didn't even know the class rules.

"We have to find out how many snacks were stolen," said Charlene. She walked to the front of the class. "I'll pass out our cards. Write down if your snack was stolen. I'll make a chart."

Charlene always had a stack of Invisible Inc. business cards with her.

"I'll help," said Sandy. She gave a card to Dawn. Dawn turned it over.

"It's blank," she said.

"Hold it up to the lightbulb by the gerbil's cage," explained Chip. "It's written in lemon juice."

Chip reached out to take the card from Dawn. Dawn drew back. She was afraid to touch Chip's invisible hands.

The gerbils were in a cage at the side of the room, and there was a light above the cage.

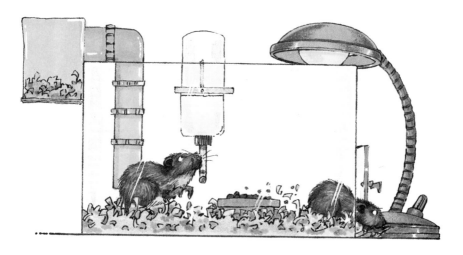

"Have you met Hola and Jambo yet?" asked Chip. "*Hola* and *Jambo* mean hello in Spanish and Swahili."

Dawn looked at the gerbils.

"Hey!" said Dawn. "One of them is getting out!"

Chip laughed and pushed Hola back into the cage.

"They're always doing that," he said.

Dawn held the card over the light. Slowly words began to appear:

INVISIBLE INC.
WE RIGHT WRONGS
COME TO US WITH
YOUR PROBLEMS.
WE CAN HELP.

CHAPTER 2
Nuts

In the cafeteria, Justin made a chart of all the snacks that had been stolen, including: Mary's nuts; Sandy's bag of raisins and nuts; Chip's peanut-butter cookies.

Justin looked up from his chart. Dawn was on the lunch line. Spaghetti was the main dish. For dessert, there was a chocolate sundae with nuts, and pudding. Dawn took pudding.

Dawn sat by herself. She looked over at the kids from Invisible Inc. Chip swallowed a strand of spaghetti. It looked like a worm flying through the air. Everybody could see the food in Chip's mouth. Chip's friends were used to it. But Dawn was not. She pushed her spaghetti

away. She wasn't hungry anymore.

Justin watched Dawn.

"Remember how Dawn was late for recess?" he said to Charlene and Chip. "Maybe she was sneaking around our classroom—"

"And taking our snacks!" said Charlene.

"She isn't eating much of her lunch," said Justin.

"Wait a minute," said Chip. "Just because she's new doesn't mean she's the thief. I think we should give her a chance."

Dawn carried her tray to cleanup. She passed Chip just as he was taking a big bite of chocolate sundae with nuts on top. A nut in a gooey puddle disappeared into his shirt. Dawn almost dropped her tray. Her pudding plopped right on Justin's head.

"Sorry," said Dawn.

"You weren't very hungry," said Justin, picking the pudding out of his hair.

"You should have had the chocolate sundae. It's much better than the pudding," said Chip.

Dawn couldn't look at Chip. He was too scary.

"I'm allergic to chocolate and nuts," said Dawn.

She hurried away.

"Ah-ha!" said Charlene. "Did you see her tray? She hardly ate a bite. She stole our snacks. That's why she wasn't hungry."

Justin shook his head sadly.

"No, Charlene. It couldn't have been Dawn," he said. He pointed to his chart. "Almost two-thirds of the snacks stolen were nuts. And Dawn is allergic to nuts."

"Nuts!" said Charlene. "I thought we had our thief. Now we have to start all over."

CHAPTER 3
A Gross Job

All week, snacks disappeared from the classroom. Invisible Inc. was busy making up its chart. Justin pointed out that snacks were stolen during both morning *and* afternoon recess.

"At least it's an equal opportunity thief," said Mr. Gonshak when Invisible Inc. showed him the chart. He taped the chart up above the gerbils' cage.

DAY	TIME	STUDENTS WITH STOLEN SNACKS
MON.	A.M.	SANDY (NUTS & RAISINS), CHARLENE (CASHEWS), MARY (NUTS) CHIP (PEANUT BUTTER COOKIES), JUSTIN (CHOCOLATE-COVERED NUTS)
	P.M.	
TUES.	A.M.	
	P.M.	KEITH (ALMONDS), MARY (OATMEAL COOKIES)
WED.	A.M.	CHARLENE (YOGURT-COVERED RAISINS)
	P.M.	SANDY (BROWNIE W/NUTS)
THUR.	A.M.	
	P.M.	

During morning recess, the teachers gathered near the play fort. Mr. Gonshak left his microphone on by mistake again.

"Teacher Lite?" said Justin.

"What are you talking about?" asked Dawn.

"Shh," said Justin. "I think I'm on to something. It might be a clue. Go get Charlene and Chip."

Dawn ran to get Charlene and Chip. Charlene and Chip knew Justin was listening to something.

"What can you hear?" asked Chip.

"The teachers are dieting together," said Justin. "They will weigh themselves today. They are going to pick the Teacher Lite of the Month."

"What does that have to do with the stolen snacks?" asked Dawn.

Justin scratched his head. He didn't have an answer.

Back inside, Mary shouted, "Somebody's been in my desk!"

The floor around her desk was a mess. Papers had fallen everywhere.

"I'll bet your snack is missing," said Charlene.

"You're right," said Mary. "I had saved my cookies from yesterday. My favorites! Ginger snaps."

Justin saw something on the floor next to Mary's desk. He got an envelope and filled it with what he found on the floor. He marked the envelope EXHIBIT A.

Just then, Mr. Gonshak came into the room.

CLASS RULES
1. No shouting out in class.
2. No calling other...
3. ...
MOTT

"We had another snack attack!" said Sandy.

"Yeah, and the mighty detectives strike out again," said Keith.

"That's enough, Keith," said Mr. Gonshak, pointing again to the respect rules.

This time, when Mr. Gonshak asked for the class motto, Dawn could shout out with the others, "Respect for ourselves and each other."

Mr. Gonshak told the boys and girls to take out their reading books. Justin pretended to read, but he was really studying Mr. Gonshak. Mr. Gonshak seemed nervous lately. He couldn't sit still. He sharpened pencils. He walked up and down the classroom.

It must be the diet, Justin thought.

Mr. Gonshak tapped on the gerbils' cage. The gerbils squeaked. A teacher on a diet wasn't easy on anybody — even the gerbils.

It was time for library. The class was working on a project about weather.

Justin slipped a note to Charlene.

I found a clue!

Justin held up the envelope.

"Do you have a signed confession?" asked Charlene.

"No, but it's a real clue." Justin emptied the envelope on the table. "I found these all around Mary's desk," he said.

"Pencil shavings!" said Charlene. "Mr. Gonshak is always sharpening pencils."

"Yes," said Justin. "And I see another clue. Look at his beard."

Mr. Gonshak was talking to the librarian, Ms. Grace. His beard was going up and down. There were crumbs stuck in it.

"Oh, gross," said Charlene.

"I bet those are ginger snap crumbs in his beard. We need to get those crumbs," said Justin. He looked at Chip. "Put them in this envelope." The envelope was marked EXHIBIT B.

"I'm supposed to pick the crumbs out of Mr. Gonshak's beard?" asked Chip. He couldn't believe it.

"It's a tough job, but somebody has got to do it," said Charlene.

Chip sighed. He raised his hand and told the librarian that he had to go to the bathroom. Then he put on his invisible clothes and snuck back into the library.

Mr. Gonshak jumped.

"Ouch!" he said.

"What's wrong?" asked Ms. Grace.

"Are there mosquitoes around here?" asked Mr. Gonshak.

Mr. Gonshak waved his hand in front of his face. He accidentally hit Chip on the nose.

"Ouch!" said Chip.

"Ah-choo!" said Charlene loudly to cover up for Chip.

One by one the crumbs disappeared from Mr. Gonshak's beard.

Then Chip changed back into his regular clothes. He held out the envelope.

"I got them!" he said excitedly.

"Good," said Justin.

EXHIBIT B

Later in the day, during science time, Justin asked the aide, Ms. Canning, if he could use the microscope.

"Sure," said Ms. Canning. "I'll be glad to help you."

She helped Justin put the crumbs under the microscope.

"Rice," said Ms. Canning.

Justin looked into the microscope. Charlene and Chip gathered around.

"Rice! Are you sure they're not cookie crumbs?" asked Justin.

"Oh, no," said Ms. Canning. "You can see the little husks from the rice kernel. This is rice. Like from those rice cakes Mr. Gonshak eats for lunch."

That afternoon, Mr. Gonshak proudly announced to the class that he had lost six pounds. He was named Teacher Lite of the Week. Invisible Inc. was wrong again.

CHAPTER 4
The Master Snacker

The next morning, the whole school went to the assembly room for the kindergarten show. It was a play about foods. Charlene's little brother, Stanley, was a turkey.

"The turkey plays a turkey," Charlene said to Chip.

During recess, Charlene looked for Stanley.

"You were a great turkey," Charlene said.

"Thanks," said Stanley. "Did you lose your snack today? You can share mine."

Stanley passed a can of nuts to Charlene. The can was labeled FANCY SALTED MIXED NUTS and it showed lots of cashews — her very favorites.

"Did Mom give you these?" she asked. "How come she didn't give these to me?"

Stanley shrugged.

"Maybe she knew somebody would steal yours," he said.

"Come on," said Chip. "Open the can. I want some, too."

Charlene twisted the lid. Suddenly, two yellow plastic snakes jumped out of the can and bopped her on the nose.

"I should have known!" Charlene shouted.

"Fooled you! Fooled you!" said Stanley. He skipped away with his friends.

"I can't believe I fell for that!" Charlene said.

"My aunt once played that trick on me," said Chip.

"Well, some detective you are," said Charlene. "Why didn't you warn me?"

"I forgot about it," said Chip.

Charlene looked thoughtful. "That brother of mine is such a sneak. I'll bet that he's our snack thief."

"Who?" asked Justin and Chip.

"Stanley!" said Charlene. "He's always having snack attacks at

home. Mom calls him the Master Snacker."

"Stanley?" said Justin. "Your little brother? You think he's been stealing the snacks in our classroom?"

"Kindergartners are so cute and little. A kindergartner could sneak into our room and nobody would notice," said Charlene.

Justin looked at Chip.

"How much skill does it take to sneak a snack?" asked Chip. "We have book buddies with the kindergarten this morning. We can check things out then."

Late in the morning, Mr. Gonshak's class went to the kindergarten class to read with their book buddies. Justin sat with Andrea, his book buddy. Andrea also had trouble hearing, and Justin was teaching her sign language. They were reading a book about caterpillars.

Andrea got up and went to her cubby hole.

"Where are you going?" Justin signed.

"Home," signed Andrea.

She pointed to the clock. Justin looked around. All the kindergartners were packing up to go home. Justin smacked his forehead with his palm.

"Morning kindergartners," he said.

Stanley put on his jacket.

"Bye-bye, Charlie-pie!" he said to his sister.

Charlene hated to be called Charlie-pie.

"You'll be a mud pie, Stanley," warned Charlene. "Just as soon as I come up with the proof that you're the one who's been taking our snacks!"

"Charlene," said Justin, "it wasn't Stanley. He's only here in the mornings. My chart shows that some of the snacks were taken in the afternoon."

"Are you sure?" Charlene asked.

"I'm sure," said Justin.

Charlene sighed. "I can't believe it. Invisible Inc. is wrong again. Where is Chip? Maybe we should just have a going-out-of-business sale."

Justin looked around. Chip was nowhere to be seen.

CHAPTER 5
An Inside Job

Back in the classroom, Dawn was staring at the top of her desk. She was holding something small, white, and round in her hand. The gerbils in the cage behind her were trying to escape again.

"Hey!" said Charlene. "That's a yogurt-covered raisin. That's my snack! What is it doing in your desk?"

"I don't know," said Dawn. "I just found it."

"Found it or took it!" said Charlene. She put her hands on her hips. "You're not allergic to raisins or yogurt. Maybe Invisible Inc. doesn't have to go out of business after all."

Dawn looked as if she wanted to crawl under her desk.

Charlene shouted. "Mr. Gonshak! Justin! Sandy! Mary! Everybody! I caught the thief. Invisible Inc. saves the day. It was Dawn, after all. I caught her with my snack in her hand."

Dawn's eyes started to fill with tears. "I didn't take it! Somebody put it in my desk. Nobody likes me. I wish I weren't me. I wish I were a big fat gerbil, like Hola and Jambo."

"The gerbils are fat because they've been eating our snacks," said a voice next to Dawn.

Dawn jumped.

"It's okay!" said the voice. "It's me — Chip. And Dawn's right. She didn't take the snacks. I came back here to hide while the classroom was empty. Hola and Jambo are to blame."

Justin ran to his desk and got the envelope marked EXHIBIT A.

"It's sawdust," he said. "Not

pencil shavings. Sawdust from the gerbil cage."

"Right!" said Chip. "It was the gerbils the whole time. They sneak out and look for food. Then they take it back to their nest to hide it under the sawdust. They dropped the yogurt raisin in Dawn's desk."

"So," said Charlene. "The snack attacks have been inside jobs. Very inside. Dawn, I'm sorry I accused you and made you cry. The next time we've got a case to solve, you can help us."

"Yeah, you're an honorary member of Invisible Inc.," said Chip.

Chip shook her hand. This time, Dawn wasn't afraid.

"Thanks!" said Dawn. "I can see that having an invisible friend can be good."

Dawn grinned. Now she had friends at her new school — and one of them was invisible.